GW00393417

THE ONE

The story of how the people of Guyana
avenge the murder of their Pasero
with help from Brother Anancy
and Sister Buxton

Other titles by the author published by Bogle-L'Ouverture Publications.

FICTION
Danny Jones. A black teenager, his friends at school, together with his parents relating to the outside world. Situated somewhere in the West of London.

Joey Tyson. One member of the Tyson family caught up during the riots of 1968 following the banning of Walter Rodney from Jamaica.

The River That Disappeared. Set in the Jamaican countryside. With the inquisitive and imaginative nine year old Lena, moonlight nights, concealed ganja cultivations as the backdrop to tragedy.

Anancy Score. Twenty original stories creatively involving Anancy in the continuing struggles of the Third World.

ANTHOLOGIES
Caribbean Folk Tales and Legends. Writing in Cuba since the Revolution. Edited and compiled.

POETRY
Jamaica. The history and more of an island people, Jamaica.

Andrew Salkey is the author of over twenty-six titles.

THE ONE

The story of how the people of Guyana
avenge the murder of their Pasero
with help from Brother Anancy
and Sister Buxton

by

ANDREW SALKEY

Published by Bogle-L'Ouverture Publications Ltd.,
141, Coldershaw Road, Ealing, London W13 9DU.

First Published in 1985 by
Bogle-L'Ouverture Publications Ltd.,
141 Coldershaw Road, Ealing, London W13 9DU

Distributed by
Bogle-L'Ouverture Publications Ltd.,
141 Coldershaw Road, Ealing, London W13 9DU

ISBN 0 904 521—32—X pbk.

Printed at the Press of Villiers Publications Ltd.,
26a Shepherds Hill,
London N6 5AH

Front cover design by John Freeman
Back cover photo Edward Cohen © 1978

FOREWORD

One-manism is the offensive and backward aspect of Caribbean politics.

In Guyana, for the past fifteen years, President for Life Forbes Burnham has been 'the one'.... Or to borrow Walter Rodney's brutally simple description, 'King Kong'. In 1980, Rodney was to die in the streets of Georgetown, capital of Guyana, a victim of a bomb attack. It is generally accepted that Rodney's assassination was executed by agents of the Burnham Regim

Rodney had become the leading opponent of the bogus 'co-operative socialist republic' that is presumably established in Guyana.

Walter Rodney was one of the Third World's leading radical intellectuals. As a historian, his book *How Europe Underdeveloped Africa* is a brilliant tour-de-force of reason, debunking much of the euro-centric view of African history.

Andrew Salkey has written a fictionalised account of the avenging of Rodney's murder. As one of the Caribbean's leading novelists and poets, he has utilised the principal folk character, Anancy.

The established perception of Anancy in our consciousness and in the writings of the Caribbean is that of a tricky spider, forever cheeky, but lovable, and inoffensive. Salkey subverts that imagery and posits the spider into the political maelstrom of Caribbean politics.

The tricky spider is removed from the generally perceived mischievous, simple, tourist smiling, folksy character and becomes a freedom fighter for justice, for real change, and against tyrants who masquerade behind the rhetoric of radical posturings.

In presenting this highly original story in Caribbean nation language, Salkey states a place for and gives further recognition to a vital and important aspect of Caribbean culture. Here Salkey exhibits the richness of argot that is alive and possesses the ability to convey subtle nuances, pathos, the serious and the comic.

The One is a welcome addition to Salkey's immense contribution to Caribbean literature. Whatever role Anancy plays in avenging the *murder* of his 'Pasero' the author is always consciously aware that the liberating process has to come from within Guyana, but that Guyana is also part of the Caribbean basin. Anancy, acting as the catalyst with help from 'Caribbea', that sea which envelops the region and knows of all our tribulations, together with Tacuma, and Sister Buxton sets in motion the process while the masses of Guyanese take to the streets to deal finally with the remnants of the corrupt regime.

The death by natural causes on August 6th of President Burnham in no way takes away from the universality of the tale. Both the remnants of the corrupt regime and one-manism remain anachronisms of Caribbean politics.

The One

The story of how the people of Guyana avenge the murder of their Pasero with help from Brother Anancy and Sister Buxton.

See nail and macca in a box of bricks, now! Poor Brother Anancy never want to go down by One Man Land for no kind of visit, at all. Him love the people them, yes. But One Man Land is one land that Anancy x-out from him mind most chiefly because as how the One Voice drowning out everybody else voice and as how the One Hand grabbing every Gawd thing that going and as how the One Power so 'pressive and brute force and terror up and dead make, morning, noon and dark night.

Yet and all, Mother Fate is a funny woman in the world. She teach lesson coming from behind so surprise you. She reach you when you least expect. And she can take you or leave you. All the same, Anancy and Fate don't take bush tea no time o' day, never was, never is. Anancy like man and woman and life that real; he not for shadow and fatalistic rungus. But see it dey, now! According to happenings, a man he respect and have plenty feelings and love for get chop down in One Man Land, and Caribbea and Brother Tacuma tell Anancy that is time that he make him next travels.

Caribbea say, 'Anancy, a travelling spiderman like you, must 'vestigate the murder that ketch you pasero in One Man Land, you know. You can't make it rest so. You got to put your spider foot right on spot and find out what wrong with a leader-man who feel that killing him own people is a correct thing to do.'

And Tacuma say, 'And listen, Anancy, try see if you can't change the leader-man ways, nuh. Or more than that, maybe? I mean, it look like him could do with a sudden pension or even a sudden, permanent holiday in some backways-moving land like Brazil or Argentina or Paraguay or nowadays Chile. See what you can arrange for the leader-man, I beg you, spiderman.'

Anancy arrive in One Man Land, three o'clock, one Friday day, sun hot. The bad politics heat bend him up, you see! Sweat rolling off him spider body like john crow bead. He suss out the heavy police and agent supervision feeling all round the airport and all the way right into Georgetown. He get the picture that say that iron fist into iron glove is how the life in One Man Land set up, from time. The One Man rule write up big, big, on everything Anancy seeing. Is like say ruffian and Party strangulation come as normal style.

He go by him dead friend headquarters, and he talk some long, old-time talk with the workers them who draw a proper history picture of the dead friend and how the One Man rule murder him. The workers tell Anancy chapter-verse concerning them Movement, the ages long One Man rule murderation of the Movement members and other people, the wicked One Man rule cover-over, the One Man Land darkness, and wha' f'do. Anancy listen good and he contemplate and he study and he re-study and he fix conclusion, and then he say to the Movement folks that he going see them, later.

As he walk outside the Movement headquarters building, he notice some shifty shanks One Man rule agents clicking camera and taking notes. Anancy feeling so much deep down contempt for the whole One Man rule that he actual walk right into the sunlight in the middle of the street and strike a bold face pose for the camera and notebook agents them. But what them didn't know is that while Anancy doing that he causing them to show themself, clear as day, and was fixing every single agent face in him spiderman memory box, click, click, click, *baps!*

Later that said afternoon, when the One Man call a meeting of the agents in him big house and garden land that he tief from the people, he begin the session like so: 'Anything suspicious in the city to report?'

The head agent lay out the Anancy pictures on the mahogany table in the centre of the sitting room, and he say, 'We got these for you, The One.'

The One Man bend down over the pictures, and he look and he look hard and he look harder, and he say, 'Who him?'

The head agent say, 'Foreigner, The One.'

The One Man suck him teet and say, 'I know that. But who him is? Him for me or gainst me?'

'Gainst you, The One, seeing as how we ketch him coming out of the Movement headquarters in broad daylight.'

'That worry me,' the One Man say. 'The broad daylight, bold face part of it, I mean. Is like he strong and don't give a fuck for iron fist in iron glove. That worry me, yes.'

'We put two, three plainclothes police on him after we take the pictures.'

'You get a report, yet?'

'Not up to meeting time with you, here, The One.'

'Send out a flash to the plainclothes police, and tell them to haul ass, up here, right now!'

The One Man walk slow round and round the mahogany table, snorting and growling and picking up and putting down all the pictures, one by one, and nodding to himself and then humming a tune that mean murderation on him mind.

In fact, the agents, who still in the sitting room, back back lickle bit when them hear the tune start up. And you know what? Them well recognize it as a coming hit tune.

The One Man stop circling the mahogany table, and ask, 'We got we own people mongst the Movement workers, right?'

'We got seven mongst them,' the head agent say.

'Get one of them to come in and report what happen when

9

the foreigner visit the Movement headquarters, today.' The One Man growl lickle bit and start to circle the mahogany table. Then he hum the tune, again.

From the time that the One Man did come back from him necessary foreign lawyer studies, years aback now, and he decide f'take up politics, he say to himself that is raw, raw power he want, more than anything else, in the whole world. Nothing else would do as substitute, *not* artist talent, *not* personality goodness, *not* even money business and personal riches. Just bull power politics!

He did join the bound-to-join struggle gainst the Englisher them, as a correct move. Then, he hux-out him friend them in that struggle and connive with two sets o' foreign rule who set him up as the favourite hemisphere sort o' leader-man. He play left. He play right. And as power tip and reach him, full, full, he decide it too sweet f'share it every four, five years with somebody else Party.

And, now, is pure power hold-on that he spend him time considering and keeping like how a next man or woman would keep keepsake and trinket.

So, you see, Anancy friend had was to get dead, mainly as how him did come on political truer and political deeper and political broader and total plural political than the One Man ever could or want to, ever, ever.

And, now, Anancy, as a foreigner sniffing round the place, was nothing but threat. And in the One Man book, threat is something that must get flick off like ticks, don't matter that the threat is a normal, good thing with Constitution standing up under it and that it popular with people and better for them than what going on from cloud top One Man rule. And is that sort o' beneficial threat that Anancy friend did signal and signify.

Meantime, Anancy put out him spider feelers and connect with the fact that plainclothes police following him everywhere he going in the city. As a master o' dodge-and-slip himself, from way, way back, he just spin round and shay-shay into a shop that sell frock and woman wig; he buy a set o' things for him wife, so him tell the saleswoman, and come out dress up different from him natural spiderman self. That happen downtown, shortly after four o'clock.

Anancy take time and start to follow the confuse plainclothes police, now.

Five o'clock come and he buck up on the happenstance of the policeman who checking out to report to the One Man. Anancy cotton on to him. He cotch up on the back of the motor car that taking the policeman to the One Man house. He look through the back window of the car and consider the plain clothes that the policeman have on and he figure that the shirt and pants could well serve a next person better, like some poor, unfortunate, honest worker-man who only have rags and tatters to go to work in. Anancy almost reach through the car window and tear the clothes off the policeman. He had was to tie down the urge, hard, hard.

Anyway, when the car arrive in the yard of the One Man house and garden land, Anancy hop off the back and run hide in some aurelia bush round the front part of the mansion.

He bend down and creep and crawl up to all the windows to get a glimpse of the session between the policeman and the One Man. He find the right window and was just in time to see another man coming into the sitting room to report. Anancy recognize him as one of the Movement workers.

The two start to give them report to the One Man. And Anancy tip up and listen good.

Then, the One Man say, 'We got to find the foreigner and clip him wing. Pick him up quick!'

11

Every man jack leave the sitting room. The One Man sit down alone. He humming the murderation tune.

Anancy studying what move he must make, now. The most definite thing he decide not to do is to change the frock and wig he got on. Is a disguise that bound to work special wonders, especial in a country and with a leader-man who don't consider woman as serious as man, woman as crafty as man, woman as threat as man, woman as human as man.

The One Man put him two hand behind him head, like two angel wing, and stretch out him two foot on the glass top coffee table that bear plenty witness to hundreds o' plait up plan-and-plot that end up eliminating scores o' obstacles to One Man rule.

Anancy make up him mind, sudden. He say to himself that is inside the house he going, don't care nothing. So, he move out o' the aurelia bush. He walk round to where the guard them stay. Then, he bow and scrape, say plenty howdy, rub him hand humble up like and praise the goodness of the One Man; and is so he manage to sneak a pass in front of one, two, three, four, five, six house guard, and begin to search real cautious for the corridor where the sitting room door connect to.

When he find it, hè stroll up to the door, and he turn and twist round the GET YOU ASS IN HERE! sign and make it say FUCK OFF AND DON'T DISTURB YOU LORD AND MASTER, THE ONE AND ONLY ONE!

Then, he open the door and call out in a proper, gentle, country-woman voice: 'I bring something nice from the Interior for you, The One! I can come in with it?'

The One Man say rough, 'How the ass you get in here, woman? Who let you in?'

'The guard them know me good, The One,' Anancy say. 'I usual come with plenty things for you and leave it with you cook, so as not to discommode you. But is the first time that I come with something that I must give you meself.'

'Awright, come in! You can't stay long, though. I busy.'

Anancy put him left hand behind him back and walk slow ginger into the One Man drawing room.

The One Man still sitting down with him foot cock up on the famous glass top coffee table. 'Put what you got for me on this table here so, and get out quick, quick!' He say all that with him two eye close, confidence father.

Anancy shake him head and smile a fox smile.

The One Man humming the murderation tune.

Same time, Anancy tighten him left fist and keep it hide safe behind him back.

The One Man two hand still making angel wing behind him head.

Anancy tiptoe round the coffee table, reach back o' the One Man chair, and lick him two time on a nerve in him neck. The One Man collapse like drop sour sop.

Anancy moving fast, now. He roll up the One Man in a real, expensive, import rug that the coffee table was standing on. As him finish doing that, the coffee table cough. Anancy look at it surprise. 'Is cough you cough?' he ask the coffee table.

'I cough, yes,' it say.

'How come?' Anancy ask.

'I's a main witness to all what go on in this room, so much so that I learn to talk because o' the heaps and heaps o' words I have to listen to, over the years and years.'

'Tell me what you know, then,' Anancy say.

'I know you not no woman. I know you is the direct foreigner them tracking, and I know how you friend get dead.'

'How it happen?'

'Them blow him up with a bomb hide inside a thing what you uses to talk with to somebody when you walking.'

'Who do it?'

'I know who order it.'

'Who?'

'The One you roll up in the rug.'

'Him same one?'

'Is him.'

Anancy lift up the rug with the One Man roll up inside it, and throw it cross him left shoulder.

'You know what time it is?' he ask the coffee table.

'Is after six o'clock,' it say.

'What usual happen round this time in the house?'

'What always happen, every minute, every day. Planning

and plotting. Setting up this, setting up that. One Man moves. Capturing something, capturing somebody. Meeting time, all the time.'

'That done, now,' Anancy say. 'New days beginning.'

'How?' the coffee table ask. 'What you going do to cause that to happen in One Man Land?'

'I going loss the One Man and him One Man rule, and you going help me do that.'

'How?'

'You going come with me and show me a good place to hide this monster of man I got drape over me shoulder.' Anancy stop and look at the coffee table, funny like. 'You can fold up, like some other table them?'

'Sure.'

'Fold up yourself, then, nuh!'

As Anancy say so, the coffee table collapse herself, sweet and easy, and shrink to the flatness of a small, small picture frame.

'I wish I could make the One Man shrink up like how you just do yourself,' Anancy say.

'Them have bush-tree leaf in the Interior that you could use to cause that to happen, you know?'

'You know where it growing?'

'Yes.' The collapse picture frame glass top coffee table start to spin herself, fast, fast.

'You checking out, somewhere?' Anancy ask anxious.

'Stay where you is, foreigner man! Don't go way! I soon come back. Hide yourself and you monster bundle back o' that bookshelf by the One Man desk! Don't move and don't make a sound until I come back!'

The coffee table spin herself, smaller and smaller, and after seconds, she fly straight through a half open jalousie blind facing the bookshelf.

As that happen so, Anancy look down on the rug and wonder to himself: *What the ass I going really do with you, eh? Which place I going put you? Which country in it right mind ever could want you? Not even Paraguay, I bet you! And though you fit f'them nasty politricks to a T, you black, and, as that is that, you salt. I feel say I should export you there, you know, make them Stroessner you to kingdom come!*

14

Some crispy crust rustling outside the sitting room door. Some voices. Then hush. After that, two swishing sound coming from the floor under the door.

Anancy peep round the bookshelf and spy two piece o' paper, fresh deliver. He tiptoe and pick them up. The first one say:

REPORT ONE

To: The One
From: Head Agent
About: The Foreigner

The Foreigner name Anancy.
Spider and man. African by origin and nature. Caribbea adopted son.
Tricky, bad. Facety. Own way.
Born to subvert. Dangerous to One Man rule.
Come to 'vestigate most recent Movement dead.

Anancy laugh quiet, when he read 'African by origin and nature. Caribbea adopted son.' He know say that the head agent do him job good. But Anancy tell himself that it would've been a perfecto job if the head agent did mention 'Tacuma best friend.' Anyhow, even the sharpest agent can miss out a direct detail, now and then.

Anancy sigh quiet, when he remember some of the things that Caribbea and Tacuma tell him to do on this said, same travels to One Man Land. '... *put you spider foot right on spot and find out what wrong with a leader-man who feel that killing him own people is a correct thing to do,*' Caribbea did say. And Tacuma, '... *try see if you can't change the leader-man ways, nuh.*'

Nail, macca and bricks, Anancy remind himself. Yet, he realize he must take a try and make possible out o' impossible.

15

He crumple up the first report, put it under him woman wig and read the second one:

REPORT TWO

To: The One
From: Plainclothes Police Chief
About: The Foreigner

The Foreigner slip we somewhere in the city. Whereabouts unknown, as yet. Could be creeping underground or swimming mongst enemy fish of One Man rule.
Still searching.

And them going search and search and search, until Roraima turn into ants hill, Anancy thinking, as he crumple up the report and hide it with the first one.

He pat the woman wig and tiptoe back across the sitting room to him hiding-place behind the bookshelf. The rug quiet. Not a move is a move. Perilventure, just in case bangarangs happen and the One Man get suffocate and dead withouten Anancy knowing, Anancy unroll out the rug and test the One Man pulse and nose breathing. Everything copasetic!

So, Anancy roll him up, again, and lodge him out o' sight. Cool breeze, Anancy whisper, and settle down to wait for as long it going take for the bush-tree leaf to reach him.

Down by the Movement headquarters, by this time, everybody get beat up and arrest. The place mash up. Nook and cranny search up. Papers and posters and books collect and grab up. Furniture splinter, and crate and drawer lay down like empty coffin outside on the sidewalk.

16

One agent talking to one plainclothes policeman, the first demon sitting down boss in a van, the other ace cotching up boasy on the fender: 'If I was head agent I would a bomb the place and blow way the Movement, one time, instead o' spending good government money on raid, search and arrest.'

'If I was chief, I wouldn't even bother arrest them; I would a just van them to a helicopter and throw them out wholesale over Kaieteur.'

That funny woman, Mother Fate, stretch out her hand as the agent and the plainclothes policeman talking them talk, and out o' the twilight shadows down a side street two half o' brick ketch each o' them headside *bup* and them sink without sound.

A next agent get pull inside a shop and turn into punching bag.

Three, four bus lose them driver and conductor and start to burn.

A whole row o' store and shop and office building losing goods and fixtures and fittings like a human swarm o' locust reach them.

Minutes, and the vengeance spreading thick all over the city.

A real, old-time, old man, who got a deep Christian word f'every Gawd thing in this Gawdless, mankind world, and who belong to the long line o' sufferers in One Man Land, hold him wife hand, lead her gentle and cautious to them upstairs front window, point to the raw beef violence going on in the street, and say to her, 'Bread on the water, Miss Vie! Look how it come back on the waves, same way it did go out, eh!'

Him wife say, 'Is stale bread, though, Josh. It take so long to come back, it stale, bad.'

'True word!' the old man say. 'Foreign soldier uses to beat we. Then f'we own police come and beat we. And we didn't do nothing. We just take it. Now, the blows floating back and police eating the same bread them dish out in prior times.' He shake him head, sad. He close the window. And he sigh a tired sigh, long as tormentation. Then he say, 'Eye f'eye, Miss Vie.'

And she say, 'Bomb f'bomb, Josh.'

17

The two o' them sit down on the sofa where them usual have old talk since forty years o' marriage. This time so, no talk. The most the wife do is pick up the old newspaper with Anancy dead friend picture on the front page, look down at it, shake her head, and sigh the same sigh her husband just sigh.

Outside a church, where prayers and hymns going on mongst a group o' woman that name Women Against Terror, some One Man Party members, army and police trouble-makers grouping up together to mash up the WAT prayers session. Them marching round and round the church yard, raising hell and shouting and chanting: 'Onward, One Man Soldiers!', 'One Man Rule, Forever!' and 'The One Will Win!'

Some army ruffians and police hooligans start to stone the church, same time.

Then, on top o' that savage ignorancy, a big belly Party member come up with a le'-go-beas' idea that the Party members, army ruffians and police hooligans must rush the church building and break up the WAT service inside. Big belly didn't even have time to finish him advice before the rush begin. Them crash the service, screaming Party slogan, throwing raw threat-abuse, and beating up some woman and man who sitting down near the aisle.

One WAT woman shout out: 'What all o' you do with the people them overseas-postal-proxy votes, the last elections? You go do the same when the One Man decide the circus must come round, again?'

As she say so, a long foot army ruffian cuff her, one time. The woman husband drop the army ruffian with a direct kick. But some four, five police hooligans rush him and beat him to the ground with baton and pitchpine stick.

Down by a street corner, near by the said church, a tall, well set-up Buxton woman who you would think is a close, tie-shin buddy o' the One Man, seeing as how the One Man ain't no stranger to the strong will village, grab hold o' one lickle fingle foot Party member, who usual torment her bout this and that, including free pussy, and drape him up by him pants belt, you see, and scrunch up him balls for all the personal bothers he cause her, especial on Saturday night time when he tek up him waters and looking easy food and rest. She have him off the ground by inches. She box him face, three, four time, and punch him good in him puff up up Party chest.

Hear him: 'You don't have no respect f'the Party, nuh, woman?'

Hear her: 'I going teach you respect for *this* party, you lickle tumpa-tail rass, you!'

And she buck him with her head, *vup, vup, vup,* and drop him in the street like mango rejec'.

Poor, fingle foot Party member! You should a see how him face fene with shock, when the Buxton woman shay-shay up to him, square off, turn round, lift up her dress, squat wide and piss all over him just-press white shirt-jack and white pants!

When she back off him, she point finger in him face and say, 'If I ever ketch you Jesus Chris' leader-man is same way I going do him.'

And is so things breaking out, minute after minute, all over the city that depress for ages under One Man rule. Is like the people ready f'independence up themself f'true. Everywhere you look, is like the people ready a'ready f'fight back, no matter how the terror strong, no matter how it long, no matter how death certain. And that is one certain that certainer than certain, in One Man Land. Dead by order of The One!

The shrink up collapse picture frame glass top coffee table fly back into the One Man sitting room, seven o'clock, exact evening time. She have a brace o' splindly bramble and leaf-spread in her mouth. She travel four different direction to pick them, nice and fresh. First, she go by Marudi. Then, she go by Amuku. Following after that, Akarai. Final point, she turn back and visit Kanuku. The special bush-tree leaf only grow by mountain shadow, and the best power come from Marudi, Amuku, Akarai and Kanuku, mountains them that stand up down by the bottom end o' the country, bud-fly distance from Brazil.

Anancy glad to see her come back. He smile a brother smile and pat the rug to make her know that things copasetic. He show her REPORT ONE and REPORT TWO, and she read them quick, dip her head this way so and that way so, and laugh a sweet beknownst laugh that could mean: *Cho, man! Don't mind that! The One Man Ben Johnson Day come, sure as fate.*

'You know what happening in the city?' she ask Anancy. 'The people revoluting gainst zuzu-wapp army and police brutality. Them mashing up the city, in a most correct and righteous way.'

'Good signal that,' Anancy say. 'In no time them bound to hook up the One Man as the true zuzu-wapp cause. We must help them connect the two 'pression into one.'

'I got the bush-tree leaf. I show you how to use it on the One Man, so you can shrink him down to pockct sizc, yes?'

'Before you do that, what name I should call you?' Anancy laugh quiet. He feel shame f'ask her such a late question, seeing how much the two o' them doing together out o' common cause and how them getting on like long-time pasero and so.

'Call me Sister Buxton, nuh! From time, I always have a deep respect for most o' the people who come from that village, you know. Them have strong will, strong mind and direct strong action. Besides that, the wood that make up me body come from a tree that grow plentiful in Buxton. You could a even consider me a Buxton native.' She clap her hand, two time, as much as to say: *That is me. I ain't nothing less. I ain't nothing more. Tek me or leave me!*

So, Anancy and Sister Buxton get down to the sitting room floor with all the bush-tree leaf-spread clock out round them. Sister Buxton strip all the leaf into a pile. Anancy break up all the woody bramble and drop them on top of the leaf pile. Then, Sister Buxton mash it with a glass ball paperweight on the One Man desk that have snow and snow flake swimming zig-zag inside it. Sudden like, Anancy noticing how the snow turning to water and wetting up the leaf and bramble pile on the floor.

20

Seconds, and is mush! Sister Buxton take up a big ashtray and put the mush inside it, careful, so none don't waste. She get up and announce to Anancy, 'It ready. Shrink you bundle and make we make a move out o' the house and garden land. Them guard soon bruck down the sitting room door.'

Anancy take up the ashtray. 'How you do it, Sister Buxton?' He sound confuse.

Sister Buxton laugh. She take the ashtray and empty it all over the rug. Then, she rub the mush into it, deep and slow.

Anancy eye nearly drop out when he see the magic effect. The rug with the One Man roll up inside it just start to shrink up, easy, easy. When it reach the size of a thing that you could put in you pocket, Sister Buxton say, 'Shrinking, I say stop!' And the rug stop shrinking, same time.

'Put it in you pocket and make we fly way!' Sister Buxton say.

'I can't fly,' Anancy say.

'Just do what I tell you, Brother Anancy!'

Anancy look sheepish doubtful.

Sister Buxton tell him to bend him knee joints, bend him two elbow like bud wing, lift up him head and tighten up him belly muscles.

'Now,' she say, 'come we go!'

And the two pasero ups and fly through the half open jalousie blind facing the bookshelf. As them do so, the sitting room door burst wide open like slice melon and house guard, head agent, army officer and police chief run inside the room shouting, 'Revolution come, The One! Wha' we must do? Give we proper guidance!'

Them don't get a Gawd answer from the One Man sitting room. It empty but just f'the furniture, bookshelf, wall pictures, table lamps, trophy things like a Texas horse saddle and the rest o' gifts to the One Man from foreigner powers.

The army officer is the only one who didn't look too surprise and didn't shout out too loud. All he do is walk round the sitting room, smiling inside him hard-hearted mind, until he come to the stretch tight, shiny, brown leather Texas horse saddle. He stand up tall beside it and put him hand on it like new owner.

21

Brother Anancy and Sister Buxton flying over the Monuments To Self spread out round the One Man house and garden land and over the One Man piranha pool and over the One Man botanical paradise property and fowl run and out over the city that revoluting with direct certainability.

The shrink up One Man stay quiet in Anancy pocket, not a whisper, not a budge.

'So, is where we going, Sister Buxton?' Anancy ask her, nice, nice, seeing as how him flying according to plan.

'Before we connect up the army and agent and police brutality to the One Man, and make the people haul down the total government, we must talk to the One Man alone somewhere quiet.'

'Like where so?'

'Mount Roraima top.'

'Why so far?'

'Because it high up and quiet, and we can pick out all the lies the One Man going tell we. Or because the highness and hush going make it hard f'him to fool we. Either which way the journey worth it.'

Brother Anancy and Sister Buxton fly over Timehri, over the Essequibo, over Bartica, over Sororieng, over Kamakusa, across to Kamarang, and south up to Mount Roraima top.

As they land down on the mystery surface that look like time-was and time-to-come-after-the-last-explosion, Anancy take the shrink up One Man out o' him pocket and set him down on a round face rock. Sister Buxton wave her hand over him eyelid and wake him up.

As the One Man looking to go on bad and prideful and facety and arrogant and nasty, Sister Buxton just step in and cut him off with: 'We capture you and shrink you down to dolly size, so hold on to you temper 'cause it could damage you. It can't do we a thing. So, calm youself!'

'What you do with me natural size?' the One Man ask.

'We make it take holiday,' Anancy tell him.

'Who you?'

'The Foreigner.'

'And who you?' the One Man ask Sister Buxton.

When she explain who she be, the One Man groan and stamp him foot, dolly style, *tumpa, tumpa, tumpa.* He vex and torment up.

'I have some question to ask you,' Anancy say. 'Is how come a leader-man like you can feel that killing him own people is a correct thing to do?'

'I don't kill nobody,' the One Man say. 'Some o' me enemies meet with a bad end, yes. Some o' me other enemies live on. And those who meet bad end, here and there, end up like that by themself. Them manoeuvre so much gainst me that them out-manoeuvre themself, right off the cliff o' politics. I don't kill people.'

'Who kill me pasero who was the Movement leader?'

'I don't know.'

'You didn't order it?'

'No. And besides, the fool was walking with a bomb that him was going to use f'loose him workers from prison, when it blow up and kill him. I can't blame for that! Him kill himself.'

Sister Buxton call Anancy, one side, and them whisper a tactics. Anancy nod yes. Sister Buxton grin a wicked grin. Then, she lift up the One Man, tie him on a stem on the end part of a tree branch, and hang him off a ledge in mid-air over Roraima.

'Awright, now,' Sister Buxton tell the One Man, 'you facing Brazil, and you can get there if I drop you nine t'ousan' foot down. You want the trip?'

'No!' the One Man say.

'Who kill Brother Anancy pasero who was the Movement leader?'

'I did order the killing.'

'Why?'

'Power reasons.'

'You mean to say that a thing like power make you do it?'

'What else powerfuller than power, Mister Foreigner?'

'Hard-to-grab things like justice and Constitution-moves

23

and human being understanding and brotherly love and tolerance-decency and so.'

The One Man don't have no answer for that. All he do instead is look down where Brazil lay down waiting for him.

'You think you could change you ways?' Anancy ask him.

'If you make me go back to me natural size and you let me go, yes,' the One Man say.

'Never!' Sister Buxton say.

'Suppose we insist you confess to all the people o' the country in a real public place in the city?' Anancy ask him.

'Well, if you...,' the One Man start to say, but Sister Buxton shut him up, pronto.

'You ain't never, never going to be you natural size, again. You going stay dolly size for the rest o' you life. Don't bargain! Don't beg!'

Sister Buxton remembering how the One Man use threat and maltreat and deceit and two-face and back track and back street and humiliate and ridicule and slap shoulder and back stab and set hand and false trap and trap door and long drop and short ketch and beat up and jive and bribe and sweet mouth and squeeze neck and rungus and ting-an'-ting so wring people life dry and pile up power under him rule like fresh-lay concrete.

Right as Sister Buxton thoughts flashing on and off, she and Anancy and the shrink down dolly One Man start to feel a rumbling and a groaning and a stumbling going on inside Roraima body.

'I think is talk Roraima want to talk,' Sister Buxton say. 'I can hear her voice making signal.'

Anancy nod a yes to Sister Buxton, and wait.

Then, after a next rumble, groan and stumble, Roraima say gentle and strong: 'I am the one woman who signify the ages and the history o' this country before it have people. I signify the time before the total continent born. From then until now, I never witness a badness worse than the badness o' this One Man you bring, here, today, to rest on top o' me head. The sooner you take him way from off me the better. The sooner you take him off the people the better. The sooner you loss him the better. That's all I want to say. Loss him! Loss him where nobody can find him!'

24

Sister Buxton look on Anancy face and Anancy do the same with a brother understanding at the smile the sister smiling, and both o' them collect up the One Man and fly way straight back to the city with him tuck safe inside Anancy pocket. And Roraima sigh relief.

She watch them disappearing through the clouds that custom to wrap round her head. And she sigh, one more time, and start to consider what she really think about the badness of the One Man. Final thing, she say to herself: *In this Indian continent, me Indian brothers and sisters and me see all kinds o' ruling and killing class o' Spanishman, Portugee, Dutchman, Englishman, Frenchman, and lately even Americanman, but this One Man come and compete with all o' them, and he don't come last.*

All during the time that Brother Anancy and Sister Buxton flying back to the city, the One Man was having some hard bob-and-weave thoughts, deep down in Anancy pocket: *But, is how I get into this position o' minus powerfulness, any at all, though, eh? Is what I do wrongful as concern me security? How come this foreigner and this piece o' furniture could a capture me and turn everything upside down? Look how I shrink down and fava man-dolly? Is what this? The one thing I know is that when I come back to me natural, I going fix them business proper. Hanging and shooting going too good for all like them. But fix them I must fix them. One Man Land is f'me property, f'me own thing, and not even Gawd Awmighty can tek it way from me. I going fix them, make direct example out o' them f'the whole country learn from. You wait!*

Same time, Anancy wondering what to do with the One Man: *I not in no mind to kill him, even though him worth it. I not going hold no trial, either. Trial too good for him. I feel say that is only one way. Loss him! Loss him somewhere else outside the people country! Roraima right. I wonder what Sister Buxton feelings is?*

25

Like Sister Buxton was hearing Anancy, she turn her head as she flying over Bartica, and she say to him, 'Anancy, we got to show the One Man for all what him is to the people them.'

'Rightful,' Anancy say. 'But how?'

'We going front him just as him is, shrink down, powerfulness minus, and throw-wayable.'

'You think the people would vex up if we throw him way?'

'No, Anancy! Most o' them would a loss him long time a'ready if them did know how. Them couldn't do it with votes, because him fix that, every election. So, with f'we suggestion and brotherly, sisterly nudging I feel say that them going plenty grateful f'true.'

'You got a plan?' Anancy ask her.

'I think so.'

Anancy consider what Sister Buxton just tell him. It copasetic. Is only one thing that bothering Anancy self. Is him foreign standing inside the people country.

So, he say to Sister Buxton, 'You know, whatever we do, you must move out front. You belong to the people. You feel the pain and tormentation that One Man rule cause. You belong. Is in you rights to change things how you want it stay. Make I just study under you as a nudger. I don't want no centre light. Awright?'

Sister Buxton smile a real nice sister smile, and say, 'I hearing you. Awright.'

Anancy smile, too, and say, 'I feel better. I feel better in me heart.'

Wonders going on in the streets. Some man and woman, who never open them mouth and say guzum-feke to duppy-catcher, opening them mouth, now, and screaming out: 'Time f'a change!' and 'Soldier, agent and police slavery must done, now!' and 'Freedom or everybody dead!'

All the One Man personality arch and monument and

public structure getting haul down and bruck up and desecrate proper.

When Brother Anancy and Sister Buxton land up in the midst o' the action in the city, them well understand that the people got them own spread-out leadership, and that them make the direct connection f'themself withouten nudging.

'The people them trump we on them own. That part o' f'we job done a'ready. I glad.' Is so Sister Buxton telling Anancy.

'I glad, too, yes,' Anancy say. 'All that leave to we f'do is show them the One Man in a public confession way.'

'Come we fly round and find a good place, and when we find it, we put out the news all over the city and the countryside and the Interior like bud-wing broadcas'.'

As soon as Sister Buxton say that, she give Anancy a sister hug, and them laugh together, turn tail, and fly way, *shoops*.

While them flying, them talking about the necessary disguise that them wearing, and Anancy say that he might as well rest the frock and woman wig and go back to him spiderman self, as per usual. Sister Buxton decide to shrink herself only when she have to fly go anywhere and look like a direct woman other times.

Up in the air, the two o' them look like twin black gaulin tuning up to sing the coming o' good weather and better times.

So, how the army, agent and police nastiness going on in the middle o' the people revolution? Well, them special nastiness not going nowhere, at all. It stop, *baps*. The higher force o' the people make the brutality dwindle fast. Soldier, agent and police turn into ordinary people, again, sudden. Them even take off them uniform, throw it way, and change how them talk and walk.

But is only one culprit who seeming to feel him could come on strong as a take-over artis', as how the One Man not on the scene and the people, according to how him seeing it, going need a next quick leader-man. Is who him? Him's the said same army officer who did stand up stocious beside the One Man stretch tight, shiny, brown leather Texas horse saddle. Is him!

And just think back, eh: that grabby-grabby, unconscionable, wicked killer-man did originate from mongst the poorest o' the poor in Albouystown bottom end, poor as gritty-gritty, not even a dutty sampata on him foot, most time nothing in him mammy pot, outside child withouten father, plenty good woman surrounding him, lickle domestic work coming in, head out a water, scarcely any sort o' schooling, army come as direct saviour.

But as time, he raise up him mind and see the world as a total kick-and-grab place, as a take-and-run market, as a kill-and-live-on parade ground. And is same way so he doing until nowadays. But the people actions cancelling out this army officer ace run.

Even now, so, he just grabalicious enough to set up three headquarters, one in him own officer office, the other one in the One Man Broadcasting Corporation, and the next one in the One Man sitting room. And he think he making big success by holding out gainst the way things going on in the streets. He got three under-officer who supporting him, and that is all. When the three o' them face him with the losing facts, he refuse blunt to give up the take-over idea. The showdown come in the One Man sitting room.

He standing up beside the stretch tight, shiny, brown leather Texas horse saddle, and he saying, 'The army is the next new government. No other!'

One supporter beg pardon and say, 'You don't have no army.'

'How come?'

'Them desert back to the people.'

'Them and the people is one,' the other supporter tell him, plain.

'Is just the four o' we leave in the army,' the last supporter say, 'and that ain't no army, no how.'

When that shrinkage o' power sink inside the army officer head, he jump up like jack and land on the saddle and start to

28

ride it right round and round the sitting room, and right out to the garden land. The three supporters run after him and take him off it and throw him in a jeep.

'Where you taking me?' the army officer ask them.

'To OMBC,' one supporter say.

'Why?'

'We got to make statement that say we's one with the people, that we's one o' them, now, part o' the revoluting. Is either that or them going kill we f'sure. And besides that, we stand a better lucky chance f'take over the government if we position weself mongst the people as one o' them, representing them interest and them new future and such like. The power leverage better that way.'

'Get the saddle!' the army officer say.

The three supporters bundle it into the jeep and them drive off to OMBC.

But see Mother Fate dey! The four o' them wasn't to reach OMBC, in no shape or form. Things contrary can happen even when things looking copasetic and planning good, as the same Mother Fate could tell you.

The jeep run out o' gas right outside the Movement headquarters. The four set o' uniform, plus the jeep, draw down a vengeance crowd. And what happen, when that happen, belong to the revolution.

And the saddle? Well, some most enterprising pickney find it cotch up gainst a lamp-post, and ride way with it.

And what happen in the short run with the army officer? Well, he get seize after the three supporters get licks and bruck head.

A most mindful Movement sister worker spy who him is, and she drag him inside the headquarters building, and she tie him up in a chair, and she send call as much Movement workers as she could muster out o' the revoluting that going on everywhere. When them gather round the army officer, not a soul say a word. The pressure o' the silence nearly break the army officer ears-drum. He start to get on nervous and maddy-maddy.

After about one minute and some seconds o' that mind pressuring, the Movement workers get the army officer to confess that is him same one who kill the Movement leader on the direct orders of the One Man. The way he say it stun all the Movement workers: 'The One Man call me in, one day, and tell me he have a special duty he want me perform f'the good o' the Republic. He say that if the Republic is to stay a good and strong Co-op Republic, then whatever and whoever threaten it must get dead. I say yes. I mean, what else I could say? So, the One Man instruc' me to build a walkie-talkie bomb thing, as him hear say that the Movement leader planning to buy that sort o' equipment for the Movement. I make friend with the Movement leader blood brother, and through him, with the Movement leader self. I tell them I believe in the workings and aspirations and action politics of the Movement, and that I can supply the walkie-talkie cheaper than cheap. I use army fixtures and I build it. I arrange the sale and hand-over. And that is how it happen, on the direct orders of the One Man.'

When he finish confess, the Movement workers lock him up in a back room, for later.

But the same sister worker, who did seize him outside the headquarters, wasn't too satisfy with the army officer confession. She figuring that he leave out some other helpful personal detail. She check back to the back room, alone, and front him with: 'Apart from the Movement leader, who else you kill mongst the Movement workers?'

'Is only the Movement leader I take orders to kill,' he say.

'That don't sound like all to me.'

'Is only him one!'

'So, who kill the two brother workers who get shoot down with nough bullet in them back, months ago?'

'That wasn't me.'

'Who, then?'

'The police did do that. Resistin' arres', them say.'

'I know the excuse. But who the policeman who kill them?'

One of those bargaining, humble pie looks dart cross the army officer face, as if to say if I tell you this you would a do that for me as a deal for a fava. The sister worker pick up on the bargaining looks but she frown it out, same time. The army officer find himself slipping fast on nothing at all, not even on sand. He duck him head like he contrite and thing.

But contrite don't mean a touch or a whisper to the sister worker. She lick him with a deep stare. He duck, again.

'I want the policeman name,' she say.

'Him name Constable Manman.'

'Right. We know him and we know where to find him. He do it under orders, too, yes?'

'Yes. On the direct orders of the One Man.'

The sister worker leave the army officer, report to the other workers, and send out a group to collect Constable Manman. When he arrive, the sister worker tie him up, question him, him confess, and she put him in the back room with the army officer.

But just before she lock the door behind her, a next light go on in her mind and she see the face of the priest-man who get knife down in a march, some time aback, and she go up to Constable Manman and ask him about it.

'I never do that,' Constable Manman say. 'That is the plainclothes police. Is them do it.'

'I want a name, Manman,' the sister worker say. 'I want name and address, right now.'

The same, identical, usual, bargaining, contrite thing happen with Constable Manman face. The sister worker deal with it dry. She stare him out. He try seconds. Nothing. And just like the army officer, Constable Manman duck him head. He mumble something.

'Name and address, Manman!' the sister worker say.

She walk round him. She staring at him. Waiting coming to her as easy as breath. She start to figure out how the One Man rule just descend on most ordinary man and woman and fling them into a different human being system where a real unmerciful nastiness like murder come out looking like plain political moves. She saying to herself: *It must change. This Manman didn't have to turn into killer. Him didn't have to bow down and follow no killer-leader. Him didn't born bad. Is this murder system that cause what happen to happen to him. The same thing with the jackass army officer. One Man rule must go!*

'Name and address, Manman!' she say, again.

Constable Manman think hard, look loss at her face, look down on the rope that tie him up tight, wait lickle bit, and

31

say, 'The plainclothes policeman name Vibert Vileman and he come from Agricola.'

Just so said, so soon done! Vibert Vileman get pick up in a cook shop in Agricola.

When he reach the Movement headquarters, the sister worker greet him with a big pretend smile and even make a joke about the wicked surname he got, and ask him just how bad him is with the people up by Agricola. Vibert Vileman reckon that the sister worker like him, and right away, he start to get on careless and boasy.

He tell her, 'F'me surname is f'me nature, yes! I don't take shit from nobody, either in Agricola or in Georgetown proper. What I say I mean I do. And what I do I does do perfec'. I's a man to me word and me surname. You like me, sister?'

'I like you, too much,' she say. 'I like you, bad, Vibert.'

'Then is why you tie me up and got me in this chair like prisoner?'

'Because I like you.'

'That don't make no sense, sister.'

'It make plenty sense, Vibert.'

'How?'

'Because I like you and want you to sit down in one place and talk to me.'

'So, you really fancy me, then?'

'Yes, I fancy you, Vibert.'

'Then why you don't free me up? Why you got me tie up like a common criminal?'

'Because that is who you is, Vibert, and because I want you to tell me about the priest-man you kill in the march.' She give him a skin-teet grin.

He get the picture. She tell him that the army officer and Constable Manman confess a'ready to what them do, and that Constable Manman name him as the killer of the priest-man.

'I do it under the direct orders of the One Man,' he say. 'I not to blame. Is orders I was following. If I didn't do it, the One Man would a fix me.'

'Like how so?'

'Him would a give a next orders f'rub me out like ink blot.'

'So, he even kill him killers, too?'

'Right. And one o' them same killer-killers would a kill me, one dark night, up in Agricola, and not a soul would a know who do it.'

Most everybody at the Movement headquarters feeling good concerning the three confession. Most everybody but not everybody! The same sister worker wondering what happening to the One Man himself. She considering her mind: *Funny how the main murder culprit, the direct devil in hell, don't get too much attention during revolution time, even from somebody like me! Is what it is about that man that even though you see him, you still see him as a kind o' invisible man, like he not mongst we, at all, while, at the same time, him foot on you neck and him gun at the back o' you head? I bet you it come down to the way him handle him One Man ruling! I bet you it funny, because he set up a baffle system that hide him while you still seeing him! Is that, yes! So, where him is, now? Now that the people raising Cain and out to bury all him relatives them, where the One Man is? Where Cain double? Is how come I never think about that before?*

Mostly, she vex with herself. She go back to the army officer. She didn't have to pressure him. She ask what she want to know, straight and easy, and the answer she get lick her hard. He tell her that the One Man missing from the house and garden land. Nobody don't know where him is.

That depress the sister worker. But not for too long. Rain have a way f'fall, when sky don't show no cloud!

Sister Buxton and Brother Anancy find a good place in Rodney Mall to hold the public meeting where them going show the One Man to the people.

Brother Anancy say, 'Maybe, we should make the announcement on two kind o' air waves?'

Sister Buxton confuse lickle bit.

Anancy explain, 'I could a do it on OMBC, and you could a fly round the country dropping the same thing in pamphlet?'

Sister Buxton laugh. 'That too sweet,' she say. 'Make we do it so, then nuh!'

The pamphlet words say: EVERYBODY TO GATHER AT RODNEY MALL BY MIDNIGHT TONIGHT TO SAY GOODBYE TO THE ONE MAN FOR EVER.

And Anancy OMBC broadcas' say: 'In the name o' the people revolution, this broadcasting station that previous use to name the One Man Broadcasting Corporation, up until today, operating now as the Voice and Face of the People. I proud to be making the first VFP broadcas' news, write personal by you own Sister Buxton....' And Anancy speak the words of Sister Buxton pamphlet, word for word, three time over, slow, slow.

When I tell you this, you see, I really mean it; the people them heart jump up like seven t'ousan' cotton ball when them hear Sister Buxton words coming out o' Brother Anancy mouth coming out o' the new broadcasting station coming out o' them radio, right there so in them room and shop and office and all 'bout. True, some Doubting Thomas folks didn't tek it in, even with sea salt, but those Didymus few. The rest o' folks believe it, and start to jubilate and spread the news like is them make it first. The whole o' One Man Land seize with a happiness that thick like cotton tree and deep as ocean pasture.

That same Miss Vie and Josh, as them cupping them ears to the old-time radio that see Englishman khaki and brown belt and stay f'see black man rule, you could feel the electric feelings running through them veins and lighting up them twin life that was stalling with fretration and depress before the news reach them.

Miss Vie say, 'Josh, the One Man time come, at last, eh?'

And Josh say, 'Every snake have him grass-piece. And grass-piece subjec' to cutting and clearance.'

Miss Vie laugh a spittle laugh, and say, 'You too good back o' the words them, Josh. Always was!'

'Is only that that poor people got, Miss Vie. Is that we rich with.' And he laugh, too.

Not all that too far from Miss Vie and Josh yard, one school pickney pitching pupa-lick outside in the street. Her mother call her. And the lickle pickney say to her jokify like, 'You don't see I playin', nah! Send One Man police f'ketch me! Send One Man army f'ketch me! Send One Man f'ketch me!'

When her mother tell her say that the One Man done and that him police and army done and that new times coming, the lickle gal pickney stop her pupa-lick, heng down her jaw, and say, 'Wha' 'appen, Mammy, the One Man *cawn* done! Somebody kill him?

The mother say, 'Better than that, chile! Like he leaving on him own. He saying goodbye, midnight tonight, up by Rodney Mall.'

'Is that what the commotion was, all this afternoon, yes?'

'And it still going on, lovey. People can tek so much, but even iron pot boil over when it stay on stove too long.'

In a next part o' Georgetown, where poverty so poor that even black bud don't land there f'fun, a man, who is a known enemy o' the One Man rule, and who usual struggle gainst the One Man, rain and shine, and who, because o' that, get beat up regular, raise up him police bruck hand in plaster, and say to him wife and son, 'I don't suppose we going ever rightly know how much money the evil bastard tief and salt way, over foreign, but is one thing though: all o' we can do with a rest from personal rule and gangsterism politics. I only hoping that all them henchman and muscleman and spy and gunman he got going go with him, wherever. If any o' them stupid enough f'stay, I, George Alan Irish, will tek care o' business, personal. Tha's one significance I promise f'do when the dust settle, maybe even before it settle good.'

'You do enough a'ready, George,' him wife, Hilda, tell him. 'You spend you whole life fighting gainst poverty and English soldier and Bookers slavery and race hatred and One Man police brutality and every Gawd imaginable thing else in this Babylon jungle that One Man politics create. Come we see how this change going work out f'we, and tek a rest, mean-time, nuh?'

'Rest is a direct thing for the unweary, Hilda,' George say, tapping out a tattoo riff on the plaster. He smile at her and shake him head. 'I too tired to stop, now.'

Them son, Erico, say, 'Papa right, Ma! All the harass and

beat he get from the One Man police and agents them cawn just go f'nothing so, because the One Man checking out. If any o' them brigidim bullyriger don't have the sense to disappear, is deal we should deal with them, same as them deal with Papa. And I know at leas' six who we owe licks.'

'I promise you, Hilda, you won't know a thing 'bout it, when we do the settlin',' George say. 'And don't fret, I have two more hand for this one that the police bruck'

George give Erico a wink, and Erico touch him mother shoulder as much as to say rest youself, Ma; poor people have power, too; Papa have me.

And, you know, is so plenty people thinking, all over the city, all through the whole country, the way One Man rule cause body injury and mind misery and loss o' life.

Some harves' bitter, yes!

Midnight come, and Rodney Mall pack up, tight, tight. As facts, the total gathering spill over every which direction far outside the Mall.

When the Movement workers hear the broadcas' over the new proclaim VFP and pick up and read the pamphlet that rain down on the street, them realize that them must produce the three.

So, standing up on the grandstand platform with Sister Buxton and Brother Anancy is the rightful human evidence that going convict the One Man, f'all time: the army officer, Constable Manman and Vibert Vileman.

Standing up behind them is the total assemble of the Movement workers. And out front, the victorious, revoluting people.

Now, is just one thing I must mention about the gathering and the event it come to witness. The going of the One Man generate a thought by some folks that say that it no more than a straight and plain going away, a real open road exit through a too easy, blinking allow sign, a getting up and a going as him did always get up and go over people with him brute force and ignorancy, a walk through a people door, just so.

Now, you see, this offend some people, you know! It offend them sense o' history, o' life, o' everyday meaning o' things.

And that is why those people standing inside and outside Rodney Mall, patient like, to see that the going of the One Man have some history lesson, some deepness and some everyday meaning for them life.

The others? Well, them dey dey just to see if it was really true that the One Man could a ever get ketch and find himself in a situation like this. That good, too.

Awright! Now, according to a prior plan mongst Sister Buxton, Brother Anancy and the sister worker from the Movement, the three killers must testify first, then Sister Buxton going produce the One Man in shrink down form and make him confess, and then, after that, the people going decide what to do with him, edification through exile or no exile, no edification.

As the minutes passing and the testifying going on, the people gasping when them hearing the wickedness coming from the army officer.

The same thing happening when Constable Manman talking.

Brother Anancy back-back from off the platform and call Sister Buxton. He say, 'I was wondering something.'

'What, Anancy? Trouble?'

'Not exactly that. But suppose the One Man refuse to confess?'

'Well, when time come, and that happen, I got a plan for that, too.'

'True?'

'True word, Anancy!'

So, the people gasping, one more time, when them hearing Vibert Vileman testifying. Even though him backside in vice, he still talking boasy and self-important. He even add a bonus piece o' information, when he tell everybody that the One Man infiltrate seven agents mongst the Movement workers. And he name them, one by one. The sister worker write them down, for later.

When Vibert Vileman done, the sister worker collect him, collect Constable Manman and the army officer, handcuff them and pass them on to some of the trusted Movement workers for prison storage. She notice that the expose seven take off like bat wing.

Then Sister Buxton walk down to the front part o' the grandstand platform, introduce Brother Anancy as a travelling spiderman who come to 'vestigate the murderation o' him friend, the Movement leader, and who help to organize the Rodney Mall meeting, and then she call Anancy, pasero of the people revolution, and she ask him to produce the shrink down One Man from out o' him pants pocket.

I tell you! When Anancy do it, you see, the people gasp a gasp that nobody ever hear before in the history o' the country.

Even the sister worker show a big, open mouth, shoulder drop surprise.

Anancy take him time and explain how every early move get make by Sister Buxton, and what she and the sister worker and the Movement workers hoping the total gathering of the people revolution will come to concerning the One Man, exile or no exile.

'But first,' Anancy say, 'everybody out there must get a chance to put question to the One Man. He owe the whole country confession and explanation.'

Anancy lift up the shrink down One Man and rest him gentle on a ship crate in the middle of the grandstand platform.

Same time, the One Man say to Anancy in a whisper, 'I just recognize you, foreigner. I recognize you features from the pictures I sight at my house.'

'Too late,' Anancy say.

The sister worker and Sister Buxton swing a spot light direct on the One Man dolly body.

The small size of this one-time giant o' terror still baffling the gathering. In fact, some folks was saying that the One Man shrink down form making him even more dangerous looking and terrorful.

The sister worker raise her hand for hush. The total Mall quiet, now. If anybody did cough, it would a sound like Mackenzie explosion.

38

Then she say, 'First question from the people?'

A Mahaicony woman announce where she from, and say to the One Man, 'What make you oppression, brutalize and kill you own? You the son o' the devil, the devil himself, or what?'

'I never oppression, brutalize or kill nobody in the Republic,' the One Man say to her. Him voice come out about a hundred time bigger than him man-dolly body.

The gathering boo him, one time.

A next woman, who come from Berbice, ask him, 'Why you tief the people them Botanical Garden and turn it into you personal fowl run?'

'I never tief nothing in the Republic,' the One Man say. 'Every move I make is a direct constitutional move, straight up, straight down.'

The booing louder, this time.

A white hair man, who born in the Rupununi, but who grow up near Tumatumari, and who see two world war over foreign, shout out, 'You say you never oppression, brutalize or kill nobody. You say you never tief. How 'bout the bad election rigging, election after election? You never do that, either, right?'

'Never!' the One Man say.

'And I never see the terror o' two world war!' the white hair man lick back. 'And the Germans them didn't get beat, two time! And nobody never get kill in the '14-'18 war and in the '39-'45 war, because the two war never happen, like how f'you clean and fair elections did take place legal and withouten interference and rigging! Right?'

The gathering laugh like clappers.

When the sounds dwindle down, a Warrau Indian girl, who going to school in Georgetown, ask, 'I don't suppose you keep up race divide-and-rule, either? Amerindian, Puttagee, White, Chinee, Black and East Indian is all one people for a man like you, yes?'

A voice slicing in from under a tree branch near the street, a voice that seem to belong to a most well-practise preacherman, add to that, 'Out of many small and unequal streams one continuous, controllable river!'

And then, a next man voice add on top o' that, 'Six unify

39

waterflow going down to the sea and into the ocean o' the wide world!

And the Warrau girl self add, 'The same wide world that make One Man politics securer than secure off a divide-and-rule and the One Man richer and richer off a race difference!'

The One Man cough boasy, stick him two thumb under him shirt-jack armpit like a man-o'-yard lawyer, and say to all that, 'I don't consider race, no time, at all, at all. I take class, and measure everything in the Republic with that. I proud o' class-analysis. That is what I use. Never race! Never race divide-and-rule! Never race hatred! What we got, here, in this country, thanks to me, is the first-ever successful Co-operative Republic in the New World, and in the entire world, if it come to that. Amerindian, Puttagee, Chinee, Black and Coolie people, and White people, too, is all one people, where I stand up in politics, and all o' you know that for a fact.'

'*Know* scunt!' a man shout out.

'*Know* shit!' a woman say.

Then, a next woman voice, with a question-sign cutlass inside it, say, quick, quick, '*Puttagee? Chinee? Coolie?*'

And a whole section o' people chorus, 'Fuck off!'

The gathering explode. Even a blind, dumb, deaf ears One-Man-ite would a know, right dey so, that the people don't believe one single word the One Man just tell them.

The booing is pure thunder. Even the sister worker couldn't get hush when she try waving down the blast. Sister Buxton try, too; but nothing.

Funny enough, though, is the One Man himself who manage to calm down everybody. He hold up him two lickle dolly hand, wave them frantic like bicycle handle-bar windmill, get the hush, and say, 'I have some news for all o' you. I ain't going confess. I ain't going confess a Gawd thing. It don't matter what you do to me; it don't matter how much evidence o' this and that you find and broadcas'; it don't matter if you threaten to murder me, I don't have a blasted thing to confess, now and no time in the future.'

The One Man last few words get drown out by a proper water-sounding roar from the gathering, plus a high cascade o' hissing and booing and whistling and foot-stamping and some skip-skap slow, slow hand-clapping.

40

Brother Anancy look at Sister Buxton, and wink. The wink say push come to shove, yes. Sister Buxton smile and wink back. And f'her wink say shove is nothing; it can get shove way, too, one time.

'So, you ready with you emergency plan?' Anancy ask her.

'I readier than ready, a'ready,' Sister Buxton say. Then, she walk down to the middle part of the grandstand platform, lift up the shrink down One Man from off the ship crate, wave him lickle body in the air, brisk, brisk, and call out for hush.

The place more than just dead still, now. In fact, it quiet like burying ground bottom end, and I mean the real far part o' it.

Sister Buxton toss the One Man from her one hand to her other hand, then she throw him to Anancy, and Anancy catch him, bounce him, two, three time in the palm o' him hand, and sink him down gentle inside the deepness of the cloth in him pants pocket.

The gathering watching every move of what going on between Sister Buxton and Brother Anancy, on the platform. It never see anything like this before, and don't matter that is a shrink down human being the gathering looking at getting this sort o' treatment. The thing that registering is the fact that anybody could handle a terror power like common plaything. Normal size or shrink down, terror power is terror power. And look what Sister Buxton and Brother Anancy doing with it! Coo yah!

Not a body, big or small, stirring. Is nothing but hard, hard attention, staring eye, and hush. Not even Queh-Queh ritual could a beat it.

Then, Sister Buxton turn full to the gathering, spread her arms wide, and ask the people, in a soft voice, 'All o' you know where the One Man piranha pool situate?'

The gathering say, 'Yes!'

'Well, we moving from the Mall to the piranha pool, right now. Why? Because we must give the One Man a right and proper setting to make him confession in.'

As soon as Sister Buxton say that, Brother Anancy feel a whole heap o' kicking and clawing and fist-thumping going on in him pants pocket.

41

'I think he get the message,' Anancy tell Sister Buxton.

'Put you hand over you pocket,' she advise Anancy, 'and come we go. The piranha hungry and waiting. Is the last stop for the clean-cut leader. Rightful statement, yes?'

Anancy nod nice.

But some more kicking and clawing and fist work going on inside Anancy pocket, and Anancy drop him hand heavy over the opening, as a warning.

Same time so, the One Man call out in a direct lawyer voice, 'Listen to me, foreigner-man, ease up, nuh! I can make it worth a pile to you, you know. I got means. Just fumble inside you pocket, like you searching for change or something, and loose me! You won't regret it. You going go back to you country a rich man. I promise you that. Just loose me!'

'You never loose the Movement leader,' Anancy say.

'I never kill him, either,' the One Man say.

'You only plan and order it, right?'

'You don't understand power, foreigner.'

'I tell you what I understand,' Anancy say. 'I understand you kill you own. I understand that, as of now, you free paper burn. And I understand that you in the hands o' you people, and is there you staying.' As Anancy say that, he lick him pocket side, *baps.*

The One Man piranha pool was always a thing the One Man proud of, you see. He usual like to show it off to celebrity-visitor and dignitary and investor and such like foreign folks. He consider it a big man symbol treat, like say it representing more than it is. One story say that the One Man have it in him mind that him and the piranha have common ways o' doing things: both o' them cut enemy quick, deep and final.

Sister Buxton, Brother Anancy and the sister worker arrive by the poolside before anybody else. Sister Buxton and Brother Anancy fly, and the sister worker hitch a cotch with a truck driver.

42

Brother Anancy take out the One Man and hand him over to Sister Buxton.

As the One Man see the piranha pool, he say to Sister Buxton in a real authority voice, 'You committing murder, you know.'

'Murder?' she say. 'No, man! I just figuring that since you won't confess to the people you enslave and injure, I must help you confess to you favourite fish. Both o' you sharp alike and cold-bloodied alike. You bound to feel like talking the truth to them. That not murder! Is oblige we obliging you, since you won't confess to you own warm-bloodied people.'

'That is still murder,' he say. The voice don't have too much lawyer leave in it.

'Look, I know you. I been hearing and witnessing you evil ways, f'ages, in that same sitting room. I know all the pain and tormentation and loss o' life you cause the people, and some o' them you own friend and comrade, too. I know all the land and money you tief.' She shake her head in a sad way. 'Now, I know that you like when we call you The One and the One Man, and so. But you know what you name change to since the people change up you world?' She wait f'him answer. He don't say nothing. She raise him up over her head and jiggle him upside down like salt cellar. He don't say a word. 'I going tell you what you name is from now on. You name The Last One. Just so. The Very Last One.'

'Murderer!' he say, pointing him finger in her face.

'That is you other name, yes.' She twist him so, and then so, again. And she laugh. 'You think I didn't hear you bargaining with Brother Anancy, a while ago, nuh? You mean to say you have nough nerve f'try and make a bargain f'you life with the very man who friend you kill? Look at that, now! So what you think Brother Anancy come all the hundreds and hundreds o' miles down here for? Eh? He come with one thing in him mind. He come f'vestigate you and how you murder him friend. Is not everybody tek bribe, you know. Anyway, I telling you this, and I mean it: you going be The Very Last One. No more like you, after you!' Then she stop and gaze into him face. Is like she was looking at more than him face. Like she was seeing the raw history of her poor,

43

unfortunate country, crease up and puff up in front of her. Then, she say, 'I hope.'

All the Rodney Mall folks gathering round the piranha pool and round the area wide about. Everybody coming to realize that this is the final move to get the One Man to confess in public. The tension tight.

Sister Buxton take the One Man behind a thick clump o' croton bush. Is only Anancy notice the move she make. He listen good and he hear a screw top bottle sound and a noise like *go-glug, go-glug, go-glug,* pouring out over something. But Anancy get distract by the sudden chanting of the gathering: 'One Man, confess! One Man, confess you crimes! One Man, you time come!'

Next thing, Sister Buxton walk out of the thick clump o' croton bush holding the One Man high over her head. He glistening in the late midnight moonlight. *Moonshine baby, moonshine doll!*

Sister Buxton walk right up to the poolside. She take her time and lower the One Man body at a dropping angle. The gathering draw breath. Even Anancy eye wide. Same way with the sister worker.

Half a pin could a drop you would a hear it like bauxite dynamite.

'You ready to confess to the people, One Man?' Sister Buxton call out to him in a steel wire voice.

'Murderer!' the One Man shout back, and then he start to bawl like a baby.

'You ready to confess to the people, One Man?' Sister Buxton call out, again.

The One Man bawling louder. Him lickle dolly body wriggling like conger eel.

'I going ask you the same question, one last time,' Sister Buxton say, steel wire under every word she saying. 'You ready to confess to the people, One Man?'

But he don't answer. Is only bawling, sobbing and wriggling he doing.

Sister Buxton wait some seconds, and then she drop him *whoosh* into the pool. The piranha dash to the surface *swash-clix-clax-clix* and haul him down under the water.

The gathering quiet as two cemetery.

44

All of a sudden, the most impossible upside down thing happen. The piranha come up to the surface in a giant whirring machine swarm and throw back the One Man whole to Sister Buxton. Not a scratch on him!

'You see!' Sister Buxton say to the gathering. 'The One Man too poisonous even for the piranha. Them rejec' him, as well. You want a better piece o' evidence o' criminal poison and wickedness in one human being than that?'

The gathering say, 'No!'

'You could want a better confession than that?'

The gathering say, 'No!'

Meantime, the One Man wet up and glistening and numb as stone.

Sister Buxton hold him up high so everybody could glimpse him face. The moonlight washing it nice and bright.

Nobody not saying anything. Nobody moving. The piranha gone under water. The surface fava glass. But it not reflecting a thing.

Sudden so, the One Man voice coming limp out o' the shrink down, wet up, glistening, dolly mouth. It saying, 'Awright, I ready to tell all. I ready to confess.'

But is like all the people just ups and loss interest in the One Man, at last. Them moving from the poolside. Them moving out o' the area. And them going back to the city, to the countryside, to the Interior, back to a land where One Man Land gone like smoke, like memory.

Brother Anancy say to Sister Buxton, 'You manage good. What you rub him with so the piranha never take him?'

'Nuh just some raw cassareep and croton bush juice,' Sister Buxton say. 'The two o' them mix is pure poison that, you know.'

'What we going do with him, now?' Anancy ask her, puzzlement bothering him features.

'The piranha don't want him. The people don't want him. The country have revolution. I don't want him. You don't want him. I don't know what to say we must do with him.'

Right there so, the shrink down One Man repeating, over and over, 'I ready. I ready to confess. I ready. I ready to confess.'

'You think that maybe Brazil or Argentina or Paraguay or

Chile would take him?' Anancy suggest in a direct serious voice that have only a small touch o' jokify inside it.

'We could try them, yes,' Sister Buxton say. She laugh. 'One thing though, I ain't giving him back him normal size, no how. Brazil or Argentina or Paraguay or Chile going have to take him shrink down permanent. If them want, them could always put him in a demi-john bottle, in a side show, in a travelling circus, and advertise him as 'The Smallest Baddest Black Man in the World'.' She laugh, again.

'Well,' Anancy say, 'before I leave you for the home base, I must ask you what you going to do youself. Where you settling?'

'Is only one place I going, Brother Anancy, and is not to no sitting room as anybody else glass top coffee table, either. I going as a full woman to Buxton Village. I going back to the proper spirit o' me people.'

'So,' Anancy say, 'is Brazil or Argentina or Paraguay or Chile with the One Man, first, and then home to Buxton?'

'Rightful order o' business that. Yes.'

'Suppose Brazil and Argentina and Paraguay and Chile don't want the One Man, shrink down or normal size? What if the circus people can't use him? What you going do with him?'

'I suppose I could always take him home to Buxton Village with me, and turn him into a concrete top coffee table.' She laugh a sweet laugh, tuck the shrink down One Man under her right arm, wave goodbye to Anancy and the sister worker with her free left hand, and fly way south-east to Brasilia.

'That same Brazil and them other dictator country she taking him to might match him political nature,' the sister worker say to Anancy, as she looking up at Sister Buxton as she flying due south-east, 'but him blackness could cause problems, don't you think?'

'Box o' bricks, nail and macca, yes,' Anancy say. 'But a taste o' him own race medicine cawn be such a bad thing. Bitter, yes! Bad? No!'

'I feel say a next set o' rejection facing him,' the sister worker say.

'I feel so, too,' Anancy say, searching the late midnight, moonlight sky for a last trace o' him friend.

But is gone she gone, far out o' sight.

46

The last thing that Brother Anancy notice, before him 'plane take off from Timehri Airport, is a whole long convoy o' jeep and lorry and dirt truck full up with One Man ministers, civil servant, technocrat, army brass, special agent, police, curry-fava individuals, and money-making grabbers heading out to a set-aside air carrier that going transport them to green back pastures Up North.

Brother Anancy reach back home, sun hot, eleven o' clock, next day. Caribbea and Brother Tacuma waiting for him down by a wharf pier where them custom meet and talk life. Anancy appear up before them looking spruce and most dutiful duty well done.

'I hear everything, total everything, a'ready,' Caribbea tell him. 'Revoluting action can travel fast, you know, special when the spot getting on like a nowadays Haiti and a new broom sweeping in from the people. And I hear how you spiderman 'vestigating help it out, too.' She touch him face with a cool sea wave. 'So, you chest puff up for something deserving, Brother Anancy? I proud o' you.'

Brother Tacuma hug him up, and say, 'That One Man criminal hard as mora wood up to the very end, eh? Is what going happen to him, you think?'

'I can't see them dark glasses gorilla folks, government or circus, bothering to take him in,' Anancy say. 'What for?'

'So?' Brother Tacuma ask.

'So, is concrete top coffee table in Buxton Village f'life,' Anancy say.

'All the same, though,' Brother Tacuma suggest, 'the niceness that would come out o' that move is the fact that the people would always know where him is, and you friend, Sister Buxton, could keep a watchful eye on him concrete self. True?' He smile.

'True, yes!' Anancy smile, too.

'Is just one thing more I want to know, Brother Anancy,' Caribbea say. 'Who in charge o' the new government?'

'The Movement workers,' Anancy say, 'with the sister worker as the leader o' the revolutionary council who responsible to the people.'

And Brother Anancy, the travelling spiderman, wave a respectful wave to Caribbea and Brother Tacuma, and walk back up the wharf pier wondering where him next travels going take him.

When a spider, who is man, vow to travel, he just have to keep on travelling, no matter where, no matter how, no matter for how long. Is that him and the world make for.